TEA with MILK

ALLEN SAY

sandpiper

Houghton Mifflin Harcourt

Boston   New York

SANDPIPER and the SANDPIPER logo are trademarks of Houghton Mifflin Harcourt Publishing Company.

For information about permission to reproduce selections from this book, write to Permissions,
Houghton Mifflin Company, 215 Park Avenue South, New York, New York 10003.

www.sandpiperbooks.com

Library of Congress Cataloging-in-Publication Data
Say, Allen.
Tea with milk / by Allen Say.
p.   cm.
Summary: After growing up near San Francisco, a young Japanese woman returns with her parents to their
native Japan, but she feels foreign and out of place.
HC ISBN-13: 978-0-395-90495-4   PA ISBN-13: 978-0-547-23747-3
1. Japan—Juvenile fiction. [1. Japan—Fiction. 2. Homesickness—Fiction.] I. Title.
PZ7.S2744Te   1999   98-11667
{E}—dc21   CIP
AC

Printed in Singapore
TWP   10 9 8 7 6 5
4500344440

For Saito Misako Sensei

From the window in her room, the girl could see the city of San Francisco. She imagined that it was a city of many palaces. And one day her father would take her there, he had promised, riding on a paddle steamer across the shining bay.

Her parents called her Ma-chan, which was short for Masako, and spoke to her in Japanese. Everyone else called her May and talked with her in English.

At home she had rice and miso soup and plain green tea for breakfast. At her friends' houses she ate pancakes and muffins and drank tea with milk and sugar.

When she graduated from high school, she wanted to go to college and then live in San Francisco. But her parents were homesick and decided to return to Japan, which was their homeland. The daughter was sad. She did not want to leave the only home she had ever known.

Once they arrived in Japan, she felt even worse. Her new home was drafty, with windows made of paper. She had to wear kimonos and sit on floors until her legs went numb. No one called her May, and Masako sounded like someone else's name. There were no more pancakes or omelets, fried chicken or spaghetti. I'll never get used to this place, she thought with a heavy heart.

Worst of all, Masako had to attend high school all over again. To learn her own language, her mother said. She could not make friends with any of the other students; they called her *gaijin* and laughed at her. *Gaijin* means "foreigner."

The woman who taught English conversation did not seem much older than Masako. Maybe she'll be my friend, Masako thought. But the teacher refused to speak English with her. She could not teach an American, she said.

So Masako wandered around the empty schoolyard. Small singsong voices came drifting from the classroom, chanting kindergarten English. She wanted to shout at them, "I know the words you are learning! Why won't you speak to me!"

At home, Masako took lessons in flower arranging, calligraphy, and the tea ceremony. She did not understand how anyone could sit on the floor for such long stretches.

"Why do I have to do this?" she exclaimed one day. "I'm not going to be a florist or a sign painter! And I like my tea with milk and sugar!"

"You are going to be a proper Japanese lady," her mother said.

"All I want is to go to college and then have an apartment of my own."

"A young lady needs a husband from a good family."

"A husband! I'd rather have a turtle than a husband!"

"We have hired a very good matchmaker," her mother said.

On the following weekend, the matchmaker introduced Masako and her mother to a young banker and his mother. In a fancy restaurant they drank tea and ate lunch and drank more tea. Then the young couple was left alone for the afternoon. The mothers prayed for the marriage of two good families. The matchmaker dreamed of the full fee she could collect.

In the evening Masako came home fuming.

"Isn't he a charming young man?" her mother asked.

"Charming like a catfish!" Masako answered.

"His family owns the bank where he works," her mother said.

"I won't marry a moneylender!" Masako replied.

Masako could not sleep that night. Mother is determined to find a husband for me, she told herself. I could never marry someone like that. Never! What can I do?

First thing the next morning, Masako put on the brightest dress she had brought from California and left the house. As she hurried to the bus stop, the villagers stopped and stared.

"She looks like a *gaijin*!" they said loudly.

I'm a foreigner in my parents' country, she thought. And they came back here because they didn't want to be foreigners. But I wasn't born here. I should leave home and live on my own, like an American daughter.

The bus took her to the train station, and there she bought a ticket to Osaka.

It was still before noon when Masako reached Osaka. She marveled at the city.

She had not seen so many cars since leaving California. She felt as though the city noises were welcoming her — the noises of trolley bells clanging, car horns blaring, trucks rumbling! And tall buildings with windows like mirrors! Everything seemed familiar, even though she had never been there before.

And most exciting of all, she saw a department store that looked like a gleaming palace. She went in.

Once she was inside, it was Masako who stared.

There were beautiful things to buy. There were restaurants and cafés and hair salons, even a theater. Am I really in Japan? she wondered. She walked aimlessly, whispering to herself, "What if I . . . Maybe I should . . ." Her heart beat faster and faster. She felt dizzy and confused.

Finally she went up to the office and asked if there were job openings. A clerk handed her an application form. As Masako filled it out, she thanked her mother for making her attend the Japanese high school, for the calligraphy lessons.

In the evening she sent a telegram to her parents. She was going to live and work in the city. She would come and get her clothes on the weekend.

The next morning Masako returned to the department store office. No one had read her application yet, the clerk said. Masako asked to see the manager. She was very insistent. After a while, a supervisor interviewed her.

"Can you really drive a car?" he asked, looking at her application. "I've never seen a woman drive."

"Many women drive in America," she said.

"I see." He nodded and picked up his telephone.

Soon a girl appeared and took Masako to a changing room and gave her a uniform. An hour later, Masako was driving an elevator cage up and down, bowing to customers, and announcing the floors.

She rented a room in a rooming house for university students. Her parents were not happy, especially her mother. It was shameful for ladies to work, she said. Masako did not tell her she was an elevator girl.

It was not long before Masako became bored with her job. "Could I do something else?" she asked the supervisor.

"You can stand by the main entrance and bow to the customers," he said.

"Only bowing? All day long?" she asked.

He nodded.

Masako returned to her elevator. No wonder ladies don't work in Japan, she thought with a sigh.

In the afternoon, as she brought down the elevator, she noticed that a small crowd had gathered in the lobby. In the middle stood the supervisor, bowing and waving his arms at a family. Suddenly Masako flushed with excitement. The family was speaking English!

"Can I be of any help?" Masako asked from behind the crowd.

"You sound like an American," a little boy said.

"And you sound like an Englishman," Masako said.

"Thank goodness," the Englishwoman said. "Tell us where you keep your hot-water bottles and umbrellas."

"And handkerchiefs," the man added.

Masako told them, and as the smiling English family left, the supervisor said to her, "I have a new job for you."

Masako became the store's guide for foreign businessmen. She had to wear a kimono for the job. How funny, she thought, that she had to look like a Japanese lady to speak English. The odd thing was that the kimono did not seem so uncomfortable now.

After some weeks, Masako noticed a young man who joined her tour two days in a row. She saw him again on the third morning. He did not look like a foreigner, and so she said to him in Japanese, "Surely you must know every corner of the store by now."

He smiled and said to her in English, "It would give me great pleasure if you would have tea with me." She stared at him.

"I went to an English school in Shanghai," he explained. "They called me Joseph. Won't you have tea with me?"

"I would enjoy that very much," she said in her very best English, and bowed as a proper Japanese lady should.

They met later and had tea in a nearby café.

"Well, Miss Moriwaki," Joseph said, looking at Masako's business card.

"I'd like it if you'd call me May," she said. "Did you always drink tea with milk and sugar?"

"It's how we used to have it at school, with crumpets," he said.

"So what brings you to the store three mornings running?"

Joseph laughed. "I work for Hong Kong and Shanghai Bank. I was transferred here six months ago and I haven't had a real conversation since. Then I heard you speaking English at the store the other day."

"What a patient man you are," she said, laughing. "And I'm glad you came back. This is the first real conversation I've had in a whole year."

"Are you planning to stay in Japan?" May asked.

"That depends," he said. "If you have certain things, I think one place is as good as any other."

"What sort of things?"

"Oh, a home, work you enjoy, food you like, good conversation. How about you? Would you like to go back to America?"

"I think so, someday," she said. "I wouldn't have to be such a proper young lady there. I could get a job or drive a car and nobody would think anything of it."

And that was the beginning of their friendship. They often met after work and on weekends. One night in the late fall they had dinner at a restaurant they liked. After a while May noticed that she was doing all the talking and Joseph was not eating his food.

"Are you all right?" she asked. Joseph nodded but said nothing.

As they left the restaurant May said, "Tell me what's wrong."

"They are transferring me," Joseph said.

"What?"

"They are sending me to another office."

"Where?"

"Yokohama."

"No!"

They walked in silence until they came to the Kobe harbor. Finally Joseph said, "Yokohama isn't that far away."

"I'm glad it's not in China," May said. "Look, Joseph. I came here on a ship like that."

"You're thinking about San Francisco, aren't you?"

Now May looked away.

"I went to an English school because my foster parents were English."

"Foster parents? You were adopted?"

Joseph nodded. "There were six of us, all adopted and all scattered now and all looking for a home. May, home isn't a place or a building that's ready-made and waiting for you, in America or anywhere else."

"You are right," she said. "I'll have to make it for myself."

"What about us?" Joseph said. "We can do it together."

"Yes," May said, nodding.

"We can start here. We can adopt this country," he said.

"One country is as good as another?" May smiled. "Yes, Joseph, let's make a home."

So they were married in Yokohama and made a home there. I was their first child.

My father called my mother May, but to everyone else she was Masako. At home they spoke English to each other and Japanese to me. Sometimes my mother wore a kimono, but she never got used to sitting on the floor for very long.

All this happened a long time ago, but even today I always drink my tea with milk and sugar.